# THE ──

# SUG RCANE

## BOY.

Alyssia A. Reddy

# THE ADVENTURES IN DODO LAND

## A story book for kids

produced by Alessandra Reddy

This first edition of The Sugarcane Boy published in United Kingdom in 2022.

A CIP catalogue record for this book is available from the British Library.

ISBN: 978-1-8382503-1-7
Published in the United Kingdom

The SugarCane boy, a publication of TriAtis
Hillcrest House
26 Leigh Road
Eastleigh SO50 9DT

www.TheSugarcaneboy.com
www.TriAtisPublications.com

To the children of the SCB Bookclubs around the world, this is all for you.

There are many more The sugarcane Boy books & workshops available.

For a complete list visit

www.TheSugarcaneboy.com

or

www.TriAtisPublications.com

# FOREWORD

Dear Reader,

Thank you for following the adventures of Sam and Toby and for purchasing the second book in the series. The 1st book was a real success and our young readers were eager to know about the next adventures of Sam and Toby. Many children from economically deprived backgrounds have had the chance to read a book and have a book at home to read via 'The SugarCane Boy bookclubs' set up in different parts of the world specially during the covid pandemic. Being an author myself and an avid reader, I believe that reading inspires you and the more you read, the more things you will know.

SamuelTReddy.com

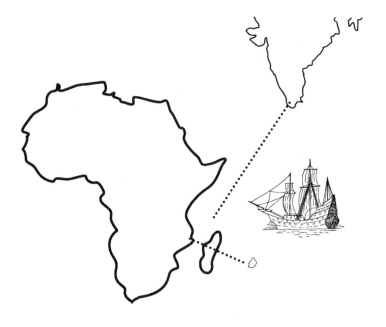

# CONTENTS

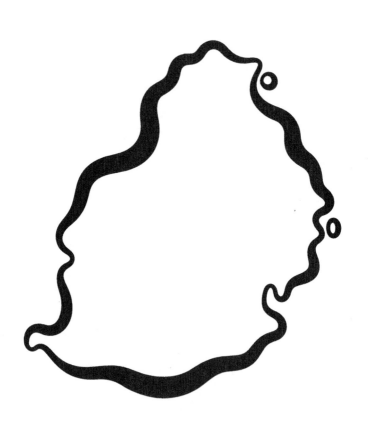

## CHAPTER 01

# INTO THE UNKNOWN

As they entered 'Caverne Hirondelle', Sam became transfixed by the intricate markings on the walls of the cave and he began to trace his fingertips over them. Though he was unable to read what they were saying, as it was all in some foreign language, he got a sense that they had a deeper meaning and that he would find out more later on. Throughout the cave, the light from the back shone brighter and brighter, which was a massive contrast with the darkness of the cave. Continuing their walk through the cave, Sam kept looking at the strange markings that were plastered on the walls, as he was filled with curiosity.

**"Toby, it looks like people wrote these on here. I wonder what else we will find!"**

**"I'm sure you'll figure it out Sam - you are a genius after all,"** Toby replied.

While walking through the cave, Sam kept stumbling on little pieces of debris that looked like they had fallen from the roof. Toby kept wandering ahead, so Sam beckoned him toward him as he bent down to pick a bit of the fallen rock. After examining it, Sam decided that the rock looked very old. However, he could see that there was something written on the stone. He blew on it and rubbed the dust away, which caused both him and Toby to have a massive coughing fit!

After the dust was out of their system, Sam desperately tried to read the markings. Nonetheless he was unable to read them, as it was too dim in there. Ploughing on, they continued on their way to the back of the cave.

Vines hung from the mouth of the cave, blocking the exit as well as the view from it. However, they could hear the faint sound of waves ahead of them, so they pushed past the vines. They reached a magnificent tree with red leaves called a flamboyant tree and a beautiful view of the sea that was almost identical to what could be seen in Mauritius.

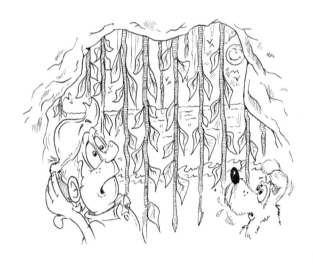

In absolute shock and awe, Sam stared at the view for a few seconds before retracing his steps back to the cave, through the vines. He emerged and retreated several times, trying to make sense of this phenomenon, as he was in complete and utter disbelief. After rubbing his eyes a few times, Sam swivelled his head toward the beach and back toward the cave, not understanding how it was all possible.

**"So, Toby, stop me if I'm wrong here but what happened was that we followed a river and it led to a magical and mysterious cave. At the other end of the cave is this beach that looks exactly like Flic en Flac, even though that stretch of the river is in the middle of Mauritius."**

With his head cocked to one side, Toby remained silent as he was probably just as confused as Sam was. Then Toby gave a bark and swiftly ran into the glistening ocean while Sam bent down and touched the grains of sand with his fingertips.

He followed Toby to the ocean and took his shoes and socks off so that he could paddle in the water. He was met with Toby jumping up and down, and it was almost as though he was a puppy again! After a few games of playing fetch with Toby and wrestling in the sand, Sam lay back on the sand and gazed at the sky while a million thoughts came into his head at once.

"**What is this place? Where is it? Is it safe here?**

**How long have we been gone? How we
even get here?"**

These were only a few of the mass of thoughts
that were swarming around in his head.

As nice as this beach was, and as much as he
was enjoying his quality time with Toby, Sam hated
not knowing the answer to his own questions.
As he was inquisitive at heart, he decided that
instead of sitting there clueless, he and Toby
would go and explore this strange place and find
out some answers for themselves! Scanning his
surroundings, he noticed that the beach was tiny
in comparison to the massive jungle that almost
swallowed up the cove.

**"Toby, come here! Let's go explore boy.
We can come back and play later."**

After brushing the sand from the soles of his feet and putting his shoes back on, they began walking further away from the sea, where they were met with a jungle of some sort.

**"A jungle by the sea!"**

Sam thought.

**"This is almost like something out of a comic book!"**

As they delved deeper into the jungle, Sam's curiosity just kept growing and growing and growing.

Suddenly they stopped and Toby began to instinctively growl. Right before them was a set of footprints... Edging closer, Toby started to sniff the footprints as Sam knelt down and examined their size. They were much bigger than his own feet but not quite as big as his dad's feet. Determined to find the source of origin of the footprints, Sam and Toby began to follow the footprints.

After what seemed like hours on end, they both paused and Sam held Toby back as his gaze drifted upwards, following what looked like smoke.

"Smoke... in the middle of a jungle? Maybe we aren't alone, Toby..."

Sam said.

Looking around Toby suddenly spoke,

"Sam, we better be careful..."

Now on high alert and with his guard up, Sam edged closer and closer towards the smoke until he was almost next to it. However, a long row of sugarcane was obscuring the view, as well as concealing them from whatever lay just beyond the sugarcane. The sugarcane was noticeably larger than the plants he knew in Mauritius.

Despite being tempted to snap a piece and put it into his pocket, he refrained and decided he would later on. As he pushed a small section of the sugarcane apart with his hands, his jaw dropped...

He seemed to have caught a glimpse of what looked like a village! However, this village was not something that he was used to... Instead of brick walls and strong roofs, he saw clay huts with straw roofs. Instead of taps and stoves, he saw a water pump and various fires lit.

What was this place...?

SUGARCANE

All of a sudden, Toby broke free from his grasp and ran into the village...

# CHAPTER 02

# BEYOND THE CAVE

Rushing behind him, Sam yelled for Toby and tried to grab him back but he was too far ahead of him. Suddenly, in front of him he saw a girl, of roughly his age, holding a jug of water. Her eyes were wide in shock. Two thick black plaits ran down her back and she had a red top and a red skirt. Quite simplistic, Sam thought.

**CRASH!.**

She dropped the jug and the water spilled everywhere as she stumbled backwards, her lips quivering and her eyes wide.

For a few moments, they stared at one another, both taking in the peculiarities of each other, before the girl broke the silence by screaming and running backwards, that caused the other children who were playing hop scotch and a marble game to stop abruptly. A swarm of people emerged from various huts with spears in their hands; unsure what to do, Sam backed away toward the bushes while desperately trying not to tremble or show fear. The crowd parted as a very tall man strode through with such confidence that he made Sam freeze to the spot.

"**Who are you?**" the man asked.

"**My name is Sam,**" he replied.

After a few moments of awkward silence, the man nodded and said.

"**Sam, you must come with me,**"

and he began to walk away.

Reluctantly, Sam followed suit while the piercing looks of a hundred strangers were fixated on him. He looked behind for Toby. Toby was busy playing with the girl that he had met earlier, so Sam followed the man into the biggest hut of all.

The inside of the hut was full of strange decorations and markings that Sam was sure he had seen before somewhere. All of a sudden, it clicked and he realised that those markings were the same as the ones in the cave. After looking around, he promptly sat down parallel to the man. In response to a swift flick of the man's hand, the three guards that Sam hadn't realised were in the room left and shut the door behind them.

For a few minutes the man stared directly at Sam while Sam averted his eyes to anywhere else in the room in order to avoid eye contact. Sensing that the man was waiting for Sam to speak, he blurted out,

**"Hi, my name is Sam and my dog is called Toby and we are from Mauritius.**

I don't know where this is or how we got here, but I promise we aren't dangerous and we are sorry for trespassing."

And then he let out a deep breath. After a moment, the man's deep frown turned into a smile and he let out a light chuckle.

"So, you're from the outside. I am the chief of the village and the girl you first met is my daughter Cami. I'm sure this is confusing for you and you must

**have many questions, but they'll all be answered soon enough,"**

the chief said.

However, Sam couldn't help but sense an ominous undertone. The chief gave Sam a nod and Sam understood that this meant he was free to go. Unsure what to do, Sam gave a swift and awkward bow which caused the chief to chuckle yet again. Rushing out, Sam began to look for Toby and saw that he was still with that girl, called Cami if he remembered correctly. As he rushed towards them, Sam couldn't help but feel a pang of jealousy: as friendly as Toby was, he was never that friendly to him.

His jealousy subsided as Cami leapt up to her feet and greeted him with the warmest smile he had ever seen as she said

**"Bonzour, ki manière? (meaning 'Good morning, how are you?').**

**My name is Cami. Your dog is so cute. What's his name?"**

**"Hi, I'm Sam and that's Toby. He really seems to like you!"**

and then just like that, they became instant friends.

As they were both playing with Toby, many kids came up to Sam in awe of his cool clothes and trendy trainers as they were just wearing handmade slippers for footwear, known as savat. Sam found himself telling stories about the outside world and answering many questions from the swarm of kids surrounding him.

Soon enough, the crowd around him began to include the adults and older people who were indulging Sam with interest in his stories and offering him food. Despite their differences, one thing that Sam was familiar with was the food, as it resembled what his mum made him.

Sam was enjoying reminiscing with tales of *'the outside world',* and he was fascinated by their responses. He still couldn't help but wonder, though, how this diverse and yet harmonious group of people had ended up here, secluded from the rest of the world and almost frozen in time.

Letting his curiosity get the better of him, he asked

**"I was just wondering, how you did end up here? "**

He was met with an uncomfortable silence followed by the villagers murmuring indistinctly with one another. Sensing the uneasiness, Cami said to Sam,

"How rude of me, I haven't given you the tour yet!"

Without waiting for an answer, she dragged him away.

## CHAPTER 03

# BONDINGS AND REALISATIONS

"I'm sorry for being so abrupt with you Sam. The past is just a sore spot around here. Even I don't know much, as all the elders refuse to tell me because they don't like talking about it,"

Cami said with a sigh.

Sam gave a nod of understanding despite still brimming with curiosity, but he decided to let it go for now. Cami continued with her tour of the village. She explained that her family had the largest hut of all as her father was the tribe chief, and that right would soon be passed on to her. She explained how all the huts were in a circle to represent equality between the rest of them and how the fireplace in the middle of the circle was used to cook large meals when they gathered as a community.

As they weaved in and out of the huts, Sam realised that each hut was marked with its own distinctive marking on the back, so he paused to examine one. Noticing his interest, she began to explain that each family has their own family crest or symbol to honour their ancestors.

"Anyway, that is enough of our boring old village. Let me show you where the REAL fun is…"

She giggled as she ran in the direction that Sam had come from, and they quickly emerged back onto the beach. The only difference was that this time the sun was fully out and casting its rays of light onto the glistening ocean – what a sight for sore eyes.

All of a sudden Toby started barking, just as Sam was walking toward the ocean. He turned around to see Cami standing by a coconut tree taking off her slippers. From the corner of his eye, he saw that the coconut tree was starting to fall, and it was going to hit her… She let out a big scream that caused the tree to shake even further. Sam yelled,

**"CAMI, RUN!!!"**

However, Cami remained frozen in fear, staring at the 10ft long coconut tree that had begun to fall on her. His instincts taking over, Sam raced toward Cami. He pushed her out of the way. With all of his inconceivable strength, he pushed the coconut tree backward so that its fall would hit the jungle instead of the beach. Then, he let out a massive sigh of relief and began stretching his contracted muscles.

As he turned to face Cami, he saw her standing there with her jaw dropped and her eyes open wide in complete and utter disbelief and shock. Realising that he had some explaining to do, he gave a small smile. Before he was able to begin, he was cut off as Cami yelled:

**"YOU HAVE POWERS TOO!!!  I HAVE POWERS TOO!!**

**Well, I'm still working on mine, but I can run super fast and I have super strength**

too. I know I was just standing there, but that happens to me sometimes. Sometimes I just get a bit scared and everyone thinks I'm making it up, but I promise I'm not,"

she waffled on, and now feeling out of breath.

Gobsmacked by that, now it was Sam's turn to stare at Cami with his mouth wide open. He barely had enough time to process it before Cami started bombarding him with questions,

"How long have you had your powers? What other powers do you have? What triggered your powers? Do you know anyone else who has these powers?"

Cami's voice began to fade in his mind as he realised that he had no idea how or why he got his powers. He only used them for a bit of fun, not thinking of the consequences or processes of how and where he got them. He just had a vague idea that he got the power from sugarcane, but he hadn't even had any of that today... With a sigh, Sam told Cami that he wasn't sure where he got his powers from, expecting her to be disappointed with him.

With a smile, Cami said

"Don't worry about it Sam. We can just go and ask the Dodo about it. It's best that he explains it to you anyway."

Sam's face contorted with confusion even more as he said,

"THE DODO<sup>???</sup>"

He was met with an equally confused look from Cami who asked him if he knew what a dodo was.

**"Dodos are extinct,"** he said.

**"Uhm, no they aren't, silly."** Cami responded.

**"Yes, they are!"** Sam said, beginning to get a bit frustrated.

**"No, they aren't, I am literally going to take you to visit him. You'll see!"** Cami retorted as she marched away.

In disbelief, Sam followed after her. What's the worst that could happen anyway? He thought to himself.

Cami confidently strode through the jungle as though she knew it all off by heart, with Sam trudging along a few steps behind her. Soon enough, they emerged in a clearing with the most beautiful waterfall that Sam had ever seen. Water cascaded down the cliff, splashing into the clear plunge pool just below.

Cami confidently walked to the waterfall and swiftly slipped behind it! Scattered around this big waterfall, were smaller waterfalls all around. Confused, Sam followed her, and that revealed that there was a secret entrance behind the waterfall. As he came out the other end he saw, in front of his very eyes, a dodo...

## CHAPTER 04

# POWER, STRENGTH AND GREATNESS

He had thought that dodos were supposed to have resembled pigeons and doves... Yet this creature was almost his height. Its feathers glistened as the water reflected upon its large and rather elegant beak.

Sam stood there, with eyes and jaw wide open once again as he attempted to speak, but he only managed to splutter a few words out.

**"Dodos... extinct... how... WHAT??"**

he mumbled, absolutely mind blown as he moved his eyes back and forth between Cami, Toby and the Dodo, who stood next to each other as though they were familiar with one another.

Collecting himself, Sam said,

**"I don't understand how this is possible... In Mauritius dodos are extinct..."**

"I know this is a lot to take in, but let me explain,"

the Dodo said in his deep voice.

"Long ago, when dodos were being hunted, we were looking for an escape and I stumbled upon this cave which led to a secret and undiscovered island . When I went to tell my family about it, I found that they had all been slaughtered. So, I came here to seek shelter and this has been my home ever since.

A few hundred years later, Cami's great great grandparents and many others also sought refuge here as indentured labourers. It is my understanding that they found another way to enter this realm through Le Morne. They have lived here ever since, as they were too scared to return in case indentured labouring was still happening."

Though rather baffled by some of this, Sam nodded as things were finally starting to make more sense to him. So this was why the village elders didn't like to talk about their past, as it was still emotionally scarring for them. What Sam couldn't comprehend was how he could understand the Dodo speaking, as he was a bird after all...

"It all makes so much more sense now, but I don't get how we can understand you. After all, you are a bird, and not to be rude..." Sam replied.

With a chuckle the Dodo said,

**"Hahaha, I feel as though it would be better for Dina to explain that."**

Sensing Sam's confusion again, he continued,

**"Dina is Cami's great grandmother and she will be able to answer all your questions. Cami knows the way from here. She will take you as I have other important matters that I must attend too. It was a pleasure meeting you, Sam!"**

As he dutifully followed Cami out once again, all these questions were racing through his mind, so he began to ask her:

"So, did you not all know that dodos exist? Why does your great grandmother live so far from you? Why couldn't the Dodo just explain it all to me?"

Cami chuckled as she said,

"We grew up thinking that there was only one dodo, you see, If the others had explained the Dodo's story to you, then they would also have had to explain our ancestry and they didn't want to do that. Granny Dina lives far away, because after my great grandad died, she inherited the position as the elder of the village. She had to live far away by the mountain to oversee the village and look after her botanical garden as well. As much as she likes being alone, Granny Dina is probably the most knowledgeable person that I know, and she has an amazing way with words! Does that answer your questions, Sam?"

Sam nodded and they continued their journey. Thick vines hung from the treetops, as light seeped through the cracks in the greenery of the leaves from above. Despite being a jungle, arrays of sugarcane were scattered everywhere, and Sam was so fascinated with them.

Soon enough, they found themself at a bridge that Cami was not familiar with crossing, as this wasn't the route she normally took. Rushing beneath the bridge was a fast-flowing river that looked lethal if they fell into it, as they would get dragged into the rocks and... Sam shuddered at the thought.

They both took it in turns to test the strength of the bridge. As flimsy as it looked, Sam and Cami began to make their way to it. All of a sudden, Toby rushed past them, leapt onto the bridge and ran to the other side with a triumphant bark. Well, that was certainly one way to do it.

Sam went first, slowly and carefully placing one foot in front of the other, fully aware of the bridge creaking beneath him.

He called out to Cami and said,

**"It looks like the bridge can only support one of us at a time, so wait until I've crossed to make your way across,"**

Almost at the other end, he realised he hadn't heard a response from Cami, so he turned around and found her just a few steps behind him.

**"CAMI!!"** he yelled, and with that the bridge collapsed...

With all his strength, Sam grabbed onto a swinging vine with one hand and  Cami's arm with his other. The bridge had given way  beneath them and the river had already washed much of it away. Cami began to swing herself. With enough force they both jumped onto the river bank.

They both sighed with relief as they got to their feet. In front of them, they saw no one other than Granny Dina. Nothing was said as she just turned around and walked in the direction of a hut close by.

**"Hi Granny, I know you told me never to go onto that bridge, but I had to this time! Oh, and this is my friend Sam. He's from the outside."**

Ominously Granny Dina said,

**"I know who you are, Sam. I saw your strength."**

With a triumphant grin, Cami gave Sam an 'I told you so' look and then sat down in front of Dina.

A few moments passed, and then Granny Dina began to speak...

"I was just a girl, but I can remember it all so clearly. We were working the land to harvest various items: sweetcorn, wheat, tea, even chillies and sugarcane. Each tribe was dedicated to harvesting something different. My tribe harvested chillies and Sam's ancestors must have harvested sugarcane. Harvesting these crops was all we could do..."

"One day, a new shipment of labourers was brought in from the mainland itself, India. Not long afterwards they revealed to us that they were in fact elite warriors from Africa, and they wished to repay us all for our kindness. They kept asking and asking us what we wanted, but we had lived a simple life as long as anyone could remember and we knew nothing different. We had no idea of the scale of power that elite warriors really had.

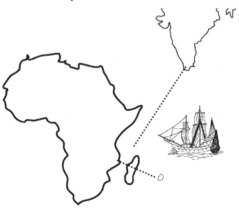

Nonetheless they persisted. They finally decreed that each of our tribes would have one worthy descendant who would gain superpowers when they were triggered by being full of emotions at one part of their life," she recalled.

"This is why Cami has powers originating from chilli, as our tribe is chilli based. The day her mother died, Cami ate lots of chilli and discovered her power. Her power can be magnified even further if she consumes more chilli, and it's similar with you, Sam. If I'm correct, you consumed sugarcane while your emotions were heightened and ever since then you have had extraordinary speed, strength and even more!" she continued.

It was as if suddenly everything clicked into place, and it all made sense to him. The only thing he was left wondering about was, if other tribes were harvesting other things, then surely...?

Grandma Dina asked if Sam and Cami were thirsty. As they were, she went to prepare them a drink from her botanical garden. A few minutes later, she returned with two mugs with steam piping from the top. Sam looked at the drink, unsure if it was some magical potion or if it was just an ordinary drink. He counted to three and then took a sip. His mouth warmed as he tasted the most delicious vanilla tea that he had ever known.

However, his happy thoughts were disturbed as the hut door opened with a bang and someone stormed in...

## CHAPTER 05

# HEROES UNITE

"CAMI! SAM! DINA!

We need to leave. NOW! "

The village has been intruded by a man with a strange weapon and he's threatening to expose our safe haven!" the village chief (Cami's father) shouted.

Cami sprinted off to the village along her normal route, with Sam alongside her. Within a flash they were back and hiding behind her family's hut. It was almost as if the vanilla tea had enhanced their superspeed. They both took turns to catch a glimpse of what was happening in the middle of the village. They could hear someone shouting,

## "SURRENDER NOW, OR FACE MY WRATH..."

The voice sounded somewhat familiar to Sam, but he just couldn't pin it down how. Taking control of the situation, Sam mustered his strength and confidently strode out to face the danger.

**"YOU leave now, or you'll face OUR wrath,"**

Sam said to the man's back. Slowly, the figure turned around, and Sam immediately recognised him. It was the man from the van, and he was holding a rifle.

**"O, boy, I know you. You're the boy that made me get fired from my job. Oh, you'll pay for that BIG time."**

He grimaced as he raised and cocked his rifle.

Sam flung himself at the man causing him to fall down, as Cami wrestled the heavy rifle out of his hand and Toby bit the man's legs. With all her strength, Cami ripped the rifle from his grasp, but not before a sharp BANG was let out. The watching villagers gasped as they were unfamiliar with this phenomenon. Thankfully, no one was hurt and Cami used the gun to hit the man on his head and he passed out. It was because of their sheer power that they were able to overcome this bad man.

A cheer came from the villagers, as the village warriors took over and bound the man's hands with rope, dragged him to a cage and locked him inside it.

Sam showed Cami how to give each other a massive high five, as the villagers began to whistle and applaud them both.

## CHAPTER 06

# SWEET SEGA AND SERENADES

Later on that evening, Sam made an announcement that he had decided to head back home - to the outside world. A wave of despair filled Cami's and all the other villagers' hearts, as they knew they would greatly miss the energetic presence of Sam and Toby. Suddenly an idea came to Cami's mind...

**"DAD, DAD! WHY DON'T WE HAVE A SEGA NIGHT IN HONOUR OF SAM?!"** Cami suggested.

Within minutes, delicious spices and smells began to waft through the air as they were being carried by the light evening breeze. First, they feasted on the food together, and then they had their Sega night. Joyous sounds came from the instruments as everyone began to clap and sing.

Sam gazed around. He had never seen such community in his life. Seeing the purity in this community was so refreshing to Sam that he decided he would not reveal this secret paradise to anyone. He must keep this a secret from the outside world.

Shortly after that, the tribe chief passed Sam a Ravane, a Sega music instrument, and so he too joined in on the fun. What made the night even more beautiful was that the festivities occurred under the flamboyant tree. The lanterns that were hung from the branches created a spectacular contrast of colours. Sam asked Cami how they managed to gather material for the lanterns and she explained how they used sugarcane for that.

Toby was having the time of his life as he ran around playing with all the children: they even tried to teach him hopscotch! Sam could hear Toby talking to the kids, but to the kids it just sounded like Toby was barking with happiness.

As the Sega night began to draw to a close, Cami made an announcement,

**"I've decided that I want to go to the outside world with Sam, I want to experience all the wonders from the outside. Sam and I are an unstoppable team, and together we can right all wrongs."**

She then turned to look at her father.

**"I promise that I will stay safe and I will return soon, Papa."**

Then, she ran to him and gave him a massive hug. He enveloped her in his arms and gripped her tightly before letting her go off into the outside world.

While Cami was saying her goodbyes, Sam saw Granny Dina beckoning him to a corner and there she whispered,

**"Deep in the sea, you and Cami will find a chest that will unlock secrets from your past. But beware, for danger follows where that chest goes..."**

Then she turned around and walked away.

The sun was setting as they both made their way towards the beach to the cave. The colours of the sun painted the sky and reflected in the ocean. It was beautiful. Sam entered the cave, with Cami following just behind him. As he walked into the cave, he kept walking deeper and deeper into it. Nothing was there! Confused, Sam walked with Cami out of the cave saying to her,

**"This is impossible."**

Looking around him, he saw that there was another cave further up the beach that he hadn't seen before; and Cami was adamant that it had never existed before either.

Nodding at Cami, he started walking towards the cave. He had a gut feeling that this cave was the one because rows of sugarcane lined the walls... As he emerged from the other end of the cave, he suddenly stopped walking as he realised, he was on a cliff edge. He put his hand behind him to stop Cami from falling as his eyes surveyed the view. They were on a mountain...

**"Le Morne?"** he questioned.

Other books in the series:

# ABOUT THE AUTHOR

Alyssia discovers her passion for writing children's book at the age of 14. She is a winning writer, finalist for the young potential award and senior prefect of her school. Her passion for books was a natural growth from reader to author. Reading is an important part of a child's development and today children as young as 6 years old in the UK are able to read out loud to their parents. Her mission is to reignite that passion in developing countries with the stories of Sam, Cami & Toby who are simple at sight and special on the inside.

Printed in Great Britain
by Amazon